the Lost Cub

5

The lost cub

iUniverse books may be ordered through booksellers or by contacting:

iUniverse
1663 Liberty Drive
Bloomington, IN 47403
www.iuniverse.com
844–349–9409

Because of the dynamic nature of the Internet, any web addresses or links contained in this book may have changed since publication and may no longer be valid. The views expressed in this work are solely those of the author and do not necessarily reflect the views of the publisher, and the publisher hereby disclaims any responsibility for them.

Any people depicted in stock imagery provided by Getty Images are models, and such images are being used for illustrative purposes only.
Certain stock imagery © Getty Images.

ISBN: 978–1–6632–3028–7 (sc)
ISBN: 978–1–6632–3029–4 (e)

Library of Congress Control Number: 2021921397

Print information available on the last page.

iUniverse rev. date: 10/21/2021

table of contents

Chapter 2. into danger

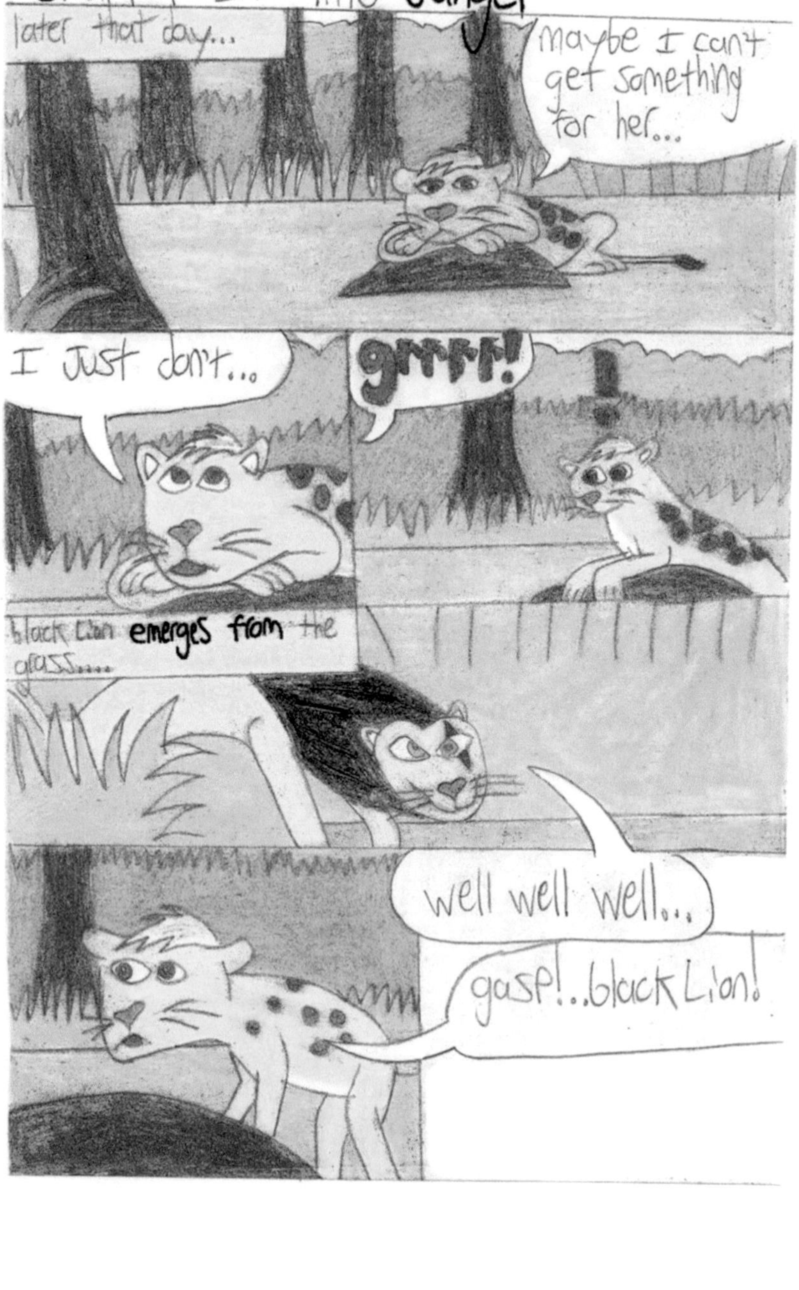

Chapter 3. a rescue Party

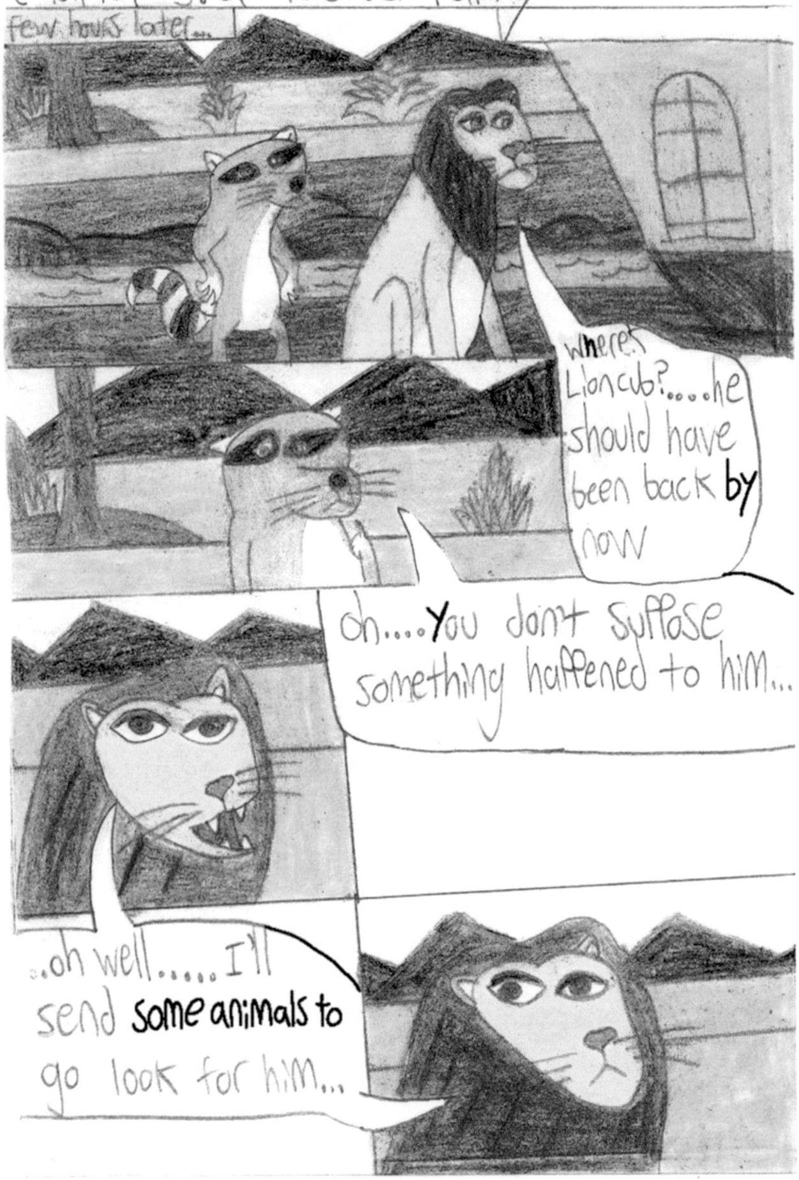

Chapter 4. a new friend

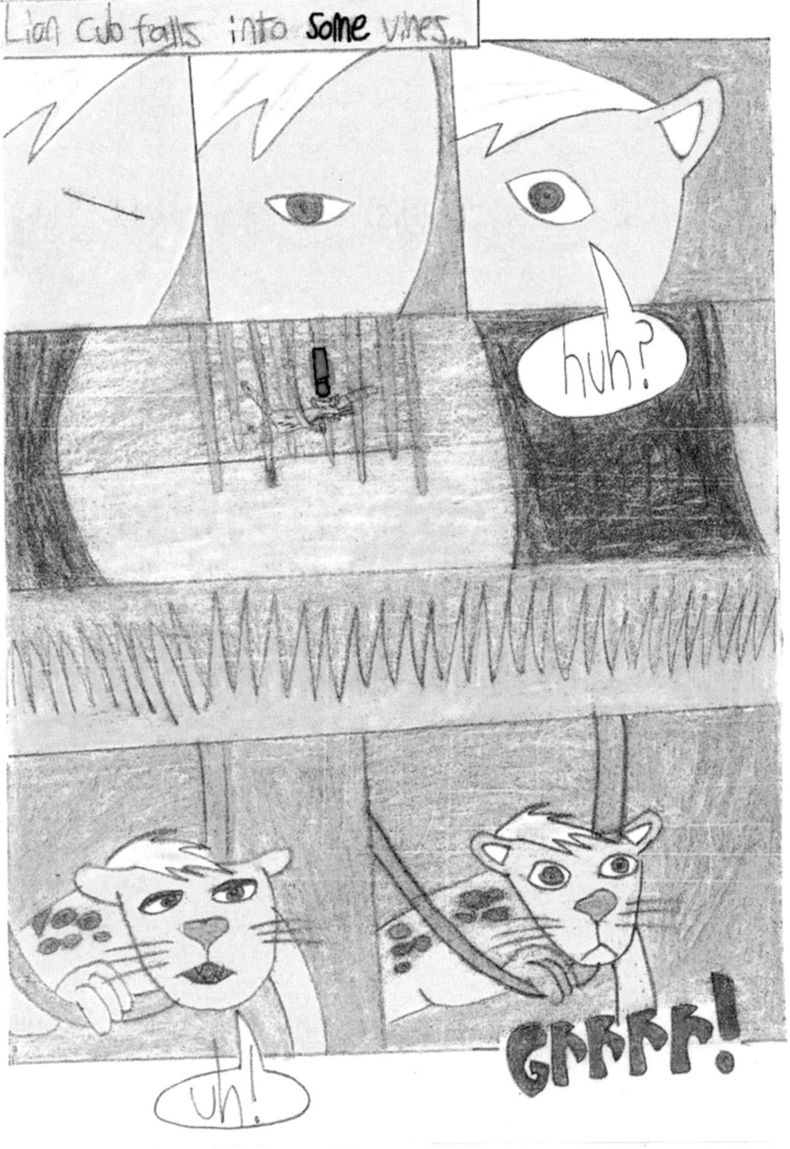

Chapter 5. Lookers become looked

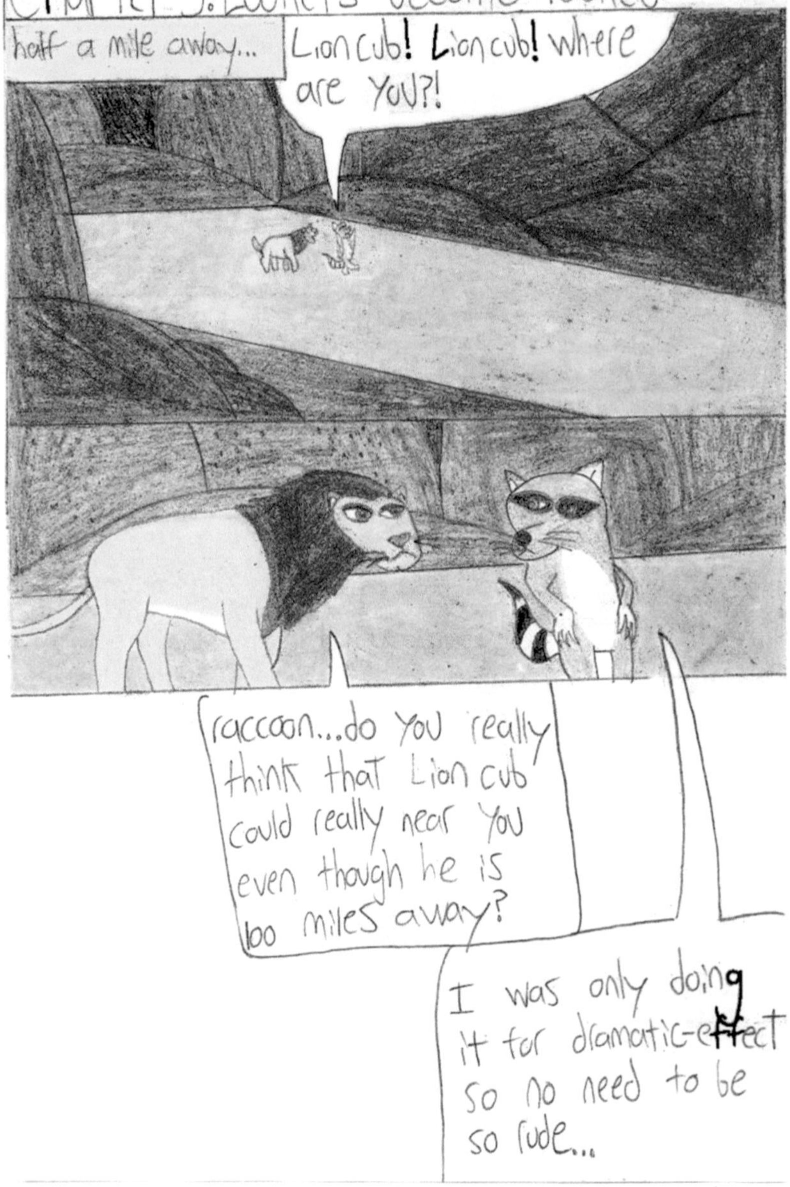

Chapter 6. A blood river

Chapter 7. foe from the beginning

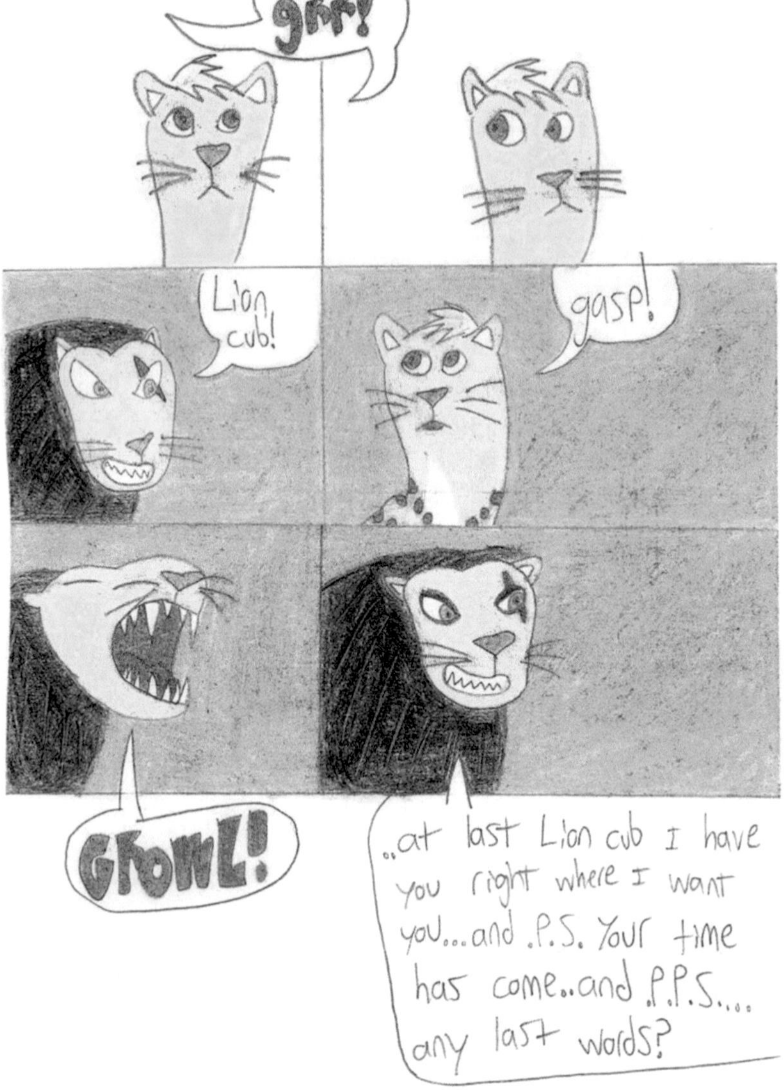

Chapter 8. friends from the beginning

all of a sudden, elephant comes out of nowhere, trumpets, and scares the daylights out of black Lion

growL!

Roar!

trooo!

chapter 9. a rainy ending

all the animals that live in the jungle take shelter in their homes...

even black lion takes shelter in his den...

The end

Printed in the United States
by Baker & Taylor Publisher Services